# My Grandparents Love Me

*With lots of love to Roger and Anne,*
*proud grandparents of Florence Grace -* **CF**

*Ai miei nonni, al nonno Garibaldi e alla nonna*
*che profumava di vaniglia, alla nonna nell'ombra*
*e al nonno elegante. Con tanto amore -* **JA**

**SIMON AND SCHUSTER**
First published in Great Britain in 2016 by Simon and Schuster UK Ltd
1st Floor, 222 Gray's Inn Road, London WC1X 8HB
A CBS Company

Text copyright © 2016 Claire Freedman
Illustrations copyright © 2016 Giuditta Gaviraghi

ISBN: 978-0-85707-585-7 (HB) • ISBN: 978-1-47117-453-7 (PB) • ISBN: 978-1-4711-4659-6 (eBook )
Printed in China • 10 9 8 7 6 5 4 3 2

# My Grandparents Love Me

Claire Freedman & Judi Abbot

**SIMON AND SCHUSTER**
London  New York  Sydney  Toronto  New Delhi

I'm off to **Gran** and **Grandpa's**,
with a big smile on my face.

I always feel wrapped up in **love**,
when I stay at their place!

Gran's big welcome **hugs** are warm.

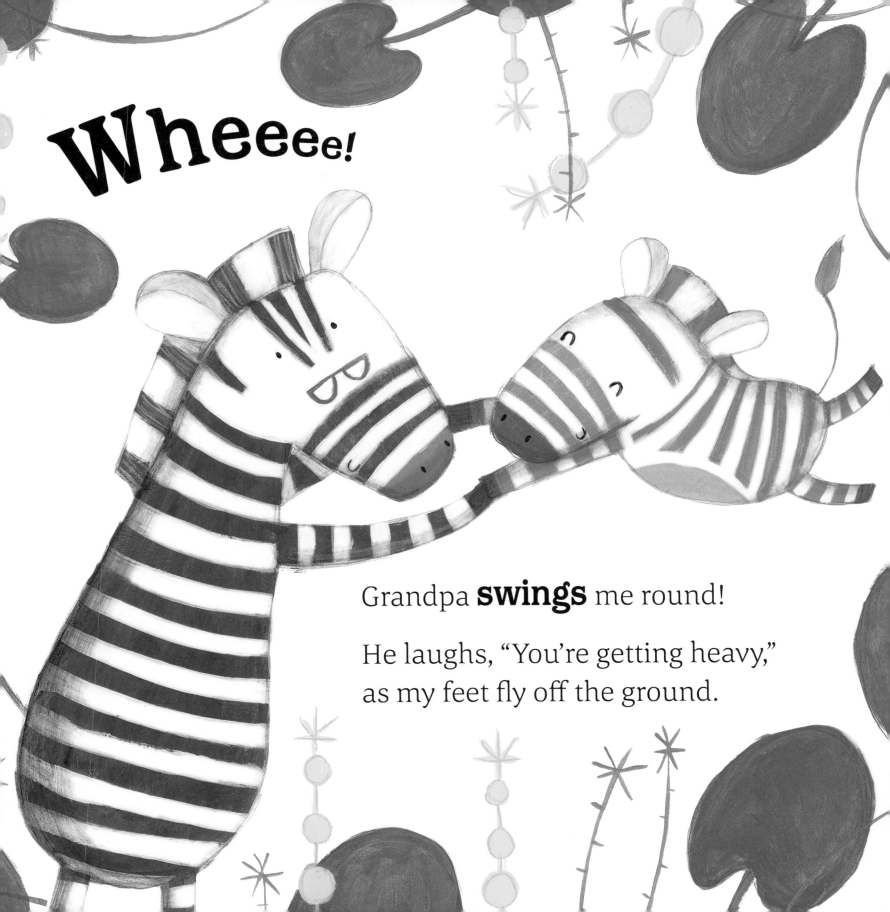

**Wheee**e!

Grandpa **swings** me round!

He laughs, "You're getting heavy," as my feet fly off the ground.

My room at Gran and Grandpa's house,
has **special** toys there too.

Gran smiles, "Have you looked on your bed?

You might find
something **new!**"

Gran's baking is delicious, **yum!**
And when I munch and scoff
more cakes than Mum would let me eat,

Gran **never** tells me off!

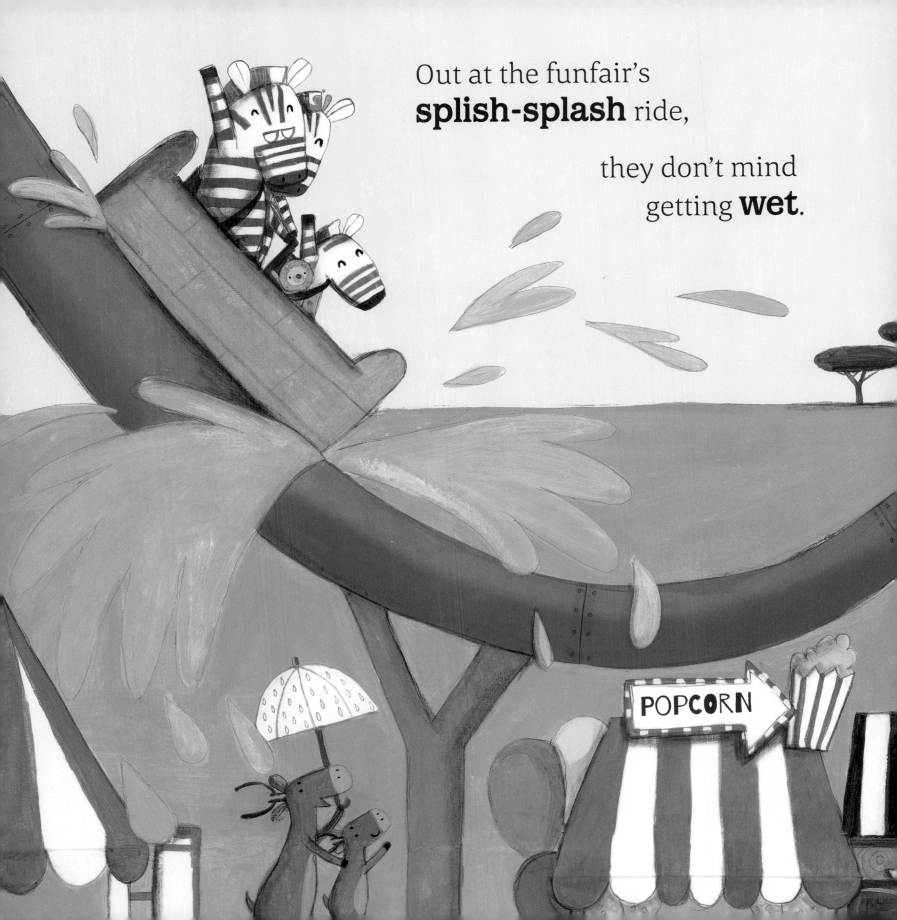

Out at the funfair's **splish-splash** ride,

they don't mind getting **wet**.

POPCORN

I don't know how Gran's handbag,
which doesn't look **that** full,

has all we need
for our day out ...

. . . it must be **magical!**

It's great to help in Grandpa's shed.
We build **amazing** things.

Gran hasn't seen our rocket —
**ssshh!**

It's red with silver wings.

Sometimes my Gran and Grandpa
will come to visit **me**.

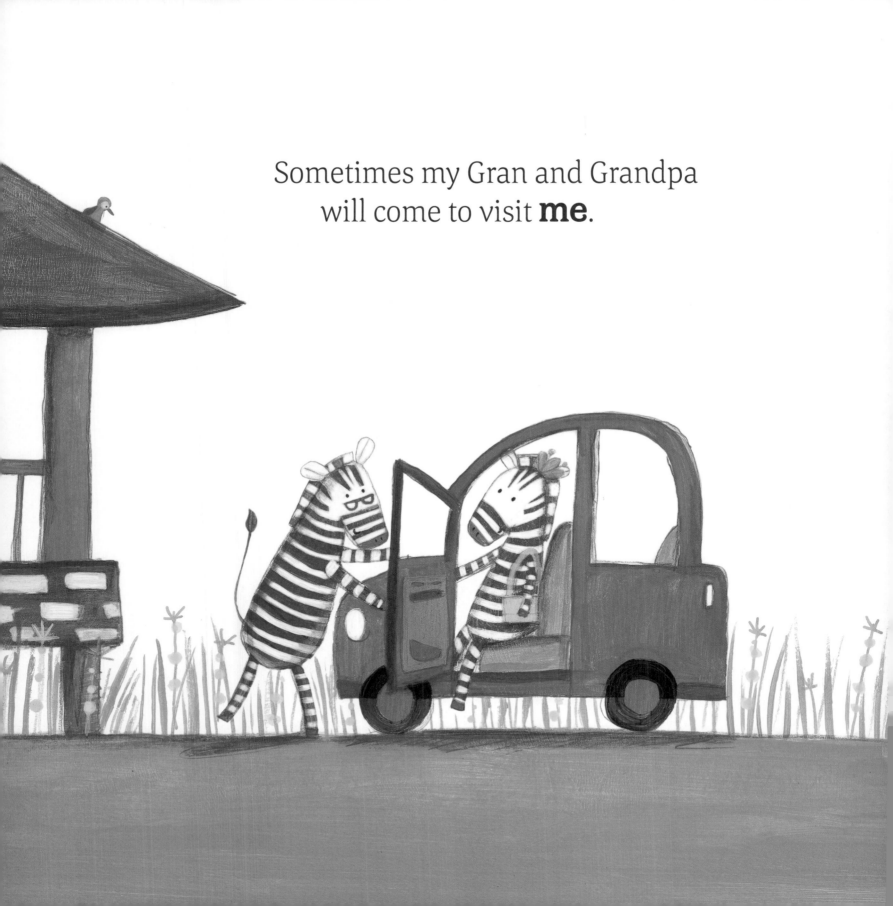

We **all** go out together then,
it's so much **fun** —
**yippeee!**

Gran says I'll be a **champion** –
she's teaching me to swim.

With her beside me, I'm **not** scared.
Now I can **jump** right in!

Back home we all dress up and dance.
Gran puts **loud** music on,

whilst funny Grandpa jokes about,
and does the steps all **wrong!**

"Let's read this story, Gran!" I say.
We **snuggle** in a chair.

Gran's silly voices make me laugh —
pretending she's the **bear!**

Warm from my bath and tucked in bed,
I yawn, "I've had such fun!"

"Us too," they smile
and kiss 'night-night'.

"We love you, little one!"